This book is for

_____

With love from

_____

On this date

_____

ZONDERKIDZ

Let's Get Ready for Bed
Copyright © 2018 by The MWS Group, LLC
Illustrations © 2018 by The MWS Group, LLC

Illustrated by Tod Carter and painted by Chuck Vollmer

Requests for information should be addressed to:

Zonderkidz, 3900 Sparks Drive SE, Grand Rapids, Michigan 49546

ISBN 978-0-310-76748-0

Design by: Diane Mielke

Printed in China

18 19 20 21 22 /DSC / 21 20 19 18 17 16 15 14 13 12 11 10 9 8 7 6 5 4 3 2 1

By GRAMMY® winner

MICHAEL W. SMITH
and MIKE NAWROCKI

Let's Get Ready for Bed

Illustrated by Tod Carter and painted by Chuck Vollmer

nurturing
steps™

"Where could he be?" said Eddy the bear.
"Have you seen Sleepy Puppy around anywhere?"
"Last time I saw him," said Lamby the sheep,
"he was heading upstairs to get ready to sleep."

"Let's go find Puppy," Eddie Bear said,
"and watch how our buddy gets ready for bed!"

A warm bubble bath is what this pup needs
after a big day of mess-making deeds.

Like splashing in mud or running around,
collecting some dust bunnies off of the ground.

He knows that a bath is the very best place
to wash jelly donuts off of his face.

Now that he's clean, he puts on his jammies,
peppered with puppies, teddies, and lambies.

Fuzzy and soft, these pj's are cozy.
They keep his toes warm and turn his cheeks rosy.

And if all his blankets fall off of his bed,
he'll have his pajamas for cover instead!

Brushing his teeth is important at night
for keeping his canines so shiny and white.

Six out of seven dog dentists agree
brushing helps puppy stay cavity-free!

A dollop of toothpaste, even if dinky,
keeps his dog breath from getting too stinky.

Then Puppy said, "Now's the time when I pray!
So I can thank God for a wonderful day."

"Thanks, God, for my family, for my mom and dad,
and for all the fun with my friends that I had."

"Please keep them safe, never out of your sight,
and help all of them to sleep soundly tonight."

Amen.

A book before bed is now what he needs,
but Puppy is too young to know how to read!

One day I will, thought Puppy, intently
turning the book's pages ever-so-gently.

He laughed at the cow jumping over the moon
and then at the dish being chased by a spoon.

Finally done with his bedtime routine,
cuddled under the covers, his teeth and fur clean,
Puppy thought for a minute he made a mistake,
"I should be tired, but I'm still wide awake."

"Did I leave something out? Or do something wrong?
I know!" he remembered. "I'm missing a song!"

Then his two friends, standing there by the door—
the two friends he hadn't noticed before,
said they would be happy to sing him a song,
"You'll be sound asleep before very long!"

"Yes, please!" Puppy said, his voice filled with bliss.
So they sang him a song that sounded like this ...

"Rock-a-bye, Puppy, in the tree top,
when the wind blows the cradle will rock.
Forward and back, the cradle it swings
'till deep into sleep, Puppy it brings."

"Rock-a-bye Puppy, do not you fear.
Never mind, Puppy, Mother is near.
Wee little paws, your eyes are shut tight.
Now sound asleep until morning light."

That did the trick, that rock-a-bye song.
And Puppy was sleeping before very long.

Then Lamby and Bear both whispered good night.
They tucked Puppy in and turned off the light.

Then quietly closing the door, Lamby said,
"Now Sleepy Puppy is ready for bed."

One of the greatest joys of my life is being the parent of five amazing kids and fourteen grandkids. Yes, fourteen. They call me G-Daddy. It is awesome. And what a great responsibility and joy to be able to pour my life into my kids and my grandkids. What a beautiful time in life for our family.

As a grandparent, I have the joy and responsibility to serve our grandkids well. That's why I created Nurturing Steps™—stories and songs that will help shape the faith of our newest generation.

I know you, your children, and grandchildren are going to love Nurturing Steps™. Generations will be blessed by your commitment.

Michael W. Smith

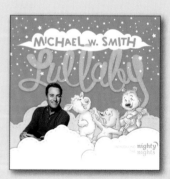

ABOUT **NURTURING STEPS**™

Founded by **Michael W. Smith**, NURTURING STEPS™ is an infant and toddler series of children's music and books with a simple mission to enliven a little one's journey with hope and faith through music and storytelling.

www.nurturingsteps.com